Opium Island

A geriatric pipe dream

This book is dedicated to Donna and Gidget. The latter can't read it and the former doesn't particularly care for it. They are deep, deep in my heart.

Preface

The Tide that Never Ends

Sinfully silent on a vacuous night the receding
tide begins,
As our minds swept clean by thoughts serene
saw the tide that never ends.
We watched the waves retreat to the night 'till
we no longer heard their roar,
And the sun rose anew, not on sparkling blue,
but on deserts that led to the shore.
Thousands were angry and millions were
scared, but you and I smiled past the shoal,
For the endless sea, so trapped and so free, had
escaped from its tedious role.
Now you and I wander these uncharted lands,
not afraid of the secrets we learn,
And the prayer that we keep as we travel so
deep is that the tide never returns.

Part 1

I felt the warmth of the sun on my eyelids. There was also a gentle rocking that reminded me that I was on the train. I listened to the rolling sound the wheels made against the steel of the track, and it seemed important, much more so than it would have not so long ago. And there were other train noises that struck me as important too, though I didn't know what they were. I felt a half-smile on my lips that often followed an evening of opium when the morning allows a little of the high to remain. I was hollow and happy.

I turned my head to shade my eyes from the sun. In front of them was the sign for the toilet. Great way to start the day. I arose from my seat cautiously, testing my knees before committing them to the walk up the isle. They were solid, and the floor was not rolling any more than one would expect. Good. I must not have taken a quay as a nightcap.

In the restroom an elderly gent in a blue long sleeve shirt was splashing water on his face.

"Hello," I said.

"Hi," he replied as he glanced at me in the mirror before him. "Do you know the name of the next town by chance?" He looked at me as though he really thought I might know. I felt I should give a little more of a reply because of that.

"No," I told him, "but I'm getting off there. I feel like walking around a little bit."

"I need to do a little gardening or something," he said.

As he turned from the sink I noticed his nametag with the word 'Brick' written on it. He looked a little stiff from too much inactivity or too much dope. It was hard to tell the difference.

"You can find gardening in any town we come to, Brick."

I felt a little chummy so I added: "I'd like to find something more in the way of cooking or waitering."

He turned to leave and added: "As early as it is, you'll probably find something you'll like."

I finished peeing and went to the sink to wash up as Brick left the compartment. I used the curiously scented soap from the metal dispenser on the sink, and washed my hands and face. There were towels aplenty in the basket to my left, so I dried off and went back to the car aisle.

Rather than sit, I walked out to the platform between cars and watched the scenery going by. A fellow was walking on the path that ran along the tracks, and he was walking darn near as fast as the train was rolling. Of course the train was only traveling eight miles per hour or so. No reason to be in a hurry. Additionally, when the whole population is old and mostly high, its nice to give folks a better than average opportunity to get out of the way.

We pulled into the station, and I noticed the name 'Bea' on the marker board held by chains above the building entry. Was this the name Bea for Beatrice, the word Bear that the critter did not allow to be finished, or was the writer just too beat to finish 'Beat'? Well, I thought, in any event this appears to be a good place to start the rest of my life.

I got in the line in front of a table that had a sign above it that read 'Bea Town Registration.' After a couple of guys in front of me got checked in properly, I stepped up and noticed a blond lady sitting behind a scanner and name sheet. She was obviously in charge of getting the new arrivals processed. I observed she had very nice breasts for a woman of her advanced age. Of course, a lot of women chose to have enhancing surgery before starting their new lives away from the great white way, but even knowing that they were visually pleasant. Her nametag said 'Nineva.'

I signed the sheet before me and placed my hand on the scanner. Nineva checked my name on the screen against my nametag and pressed a button on the scanner that read my fingerprints and barcode.

"Have a nice stay," she said as she lifted her eyes to see mine were a tad lower.

I said: "Tit's starting out well."

She briefly grinned without giving me the old 'my–eyes-are up-here' glare. That didn't make me feel particularly clever, but it was said and there we are.

Walking out into the main street, I checked out the town directory written on horizontal planks, national park style. They offered restaurants, surfing, gardening, fishing, a laundry, an opium dispensary and tavern, a lithium bar, movie theatre, art studio and the list went on longer than my attention span. Past the sign I saw a restaurant named 'Fab Foods for You' with inside and outside dining. I walked over as a mostly bald guy in a wrinkled white shirt was leaving, turning around the 'we have waiter' to the 'we need waiter' side of the window sign. I walked in and turned the sign back around and went to a table occupied by three gentlemen.

"Have you placed your order yet?" I inquired.

"We have," a guy in a blue shirt and a ruddy complexion replied.

The others at the table looked out the window and were probably a little high. I guessed blue shirt was their designated communicator.

I told them I would check on it.

I walked to the kitchen window and saw a plump old guy in a chef's hat turning some eggs and bacon.

I told him I was the new waiter and to holler when the order was ready and then asked what else I could do.

"Get some bread out of the fridge and toast up eight pieces, six for them and two for me," he said without looking up from the stovetop.

I did as requested, and took the finished plates to the table.

I told blue shirt and his pals to just leave the plates on the table when they were finished. The two stoned dudes trusted themselves to say thanks. I said that they were welcome. Using the phrase 'no problem' is strictly forbidden here. It is apparently too stoner sounding even among frequent fliers.

I toasted two more bread slices for me and had the chef fry some bacon for a BLT. The tomatoes in the basket on the counter looked great. Being home grown, they always were.

Finishing my sandwich, I walked out of the café, turning the window sign back to 'we need waiter.'

Still being pretty early in the day, not knowing or caring exactly what time it was, I moseyed over to the tavern area to do a little high living. Not wanting to make a full day of sailing on opium, I skipped on past that bar to the lithium hangout. I pushed around the rotating entry door and found a half lighted room with twelve or so men sitting around visiting in small groups. One old dude was going through the record albums by the stereo. Having selected one, he spun what turned out to be some nice instrumental west coast jazz from the fifties. The lithium canister was hissing lightly in the center of the room. Everyone was grinning ear-to-ear from the gas, and chatting like teenage girls on a Friday afternoon. I immediately fell into the feeling and took a seat by the phono man.

I told him that I thought it was a great day for jazz.

"Every day is," was his good-natured reply.

He looked at my nametag and said: "You know, Glendale, they really did a nice job of laying in the sound equipment here... Not exactly audiophile, but top notch entry level and easy to use. They even have spare styli behind the bar for when old hands drop the tone arm from too high too often."

I nodded and replied.

"I sent all my albums over here before I came. I couldn't tell them where to put them exactly, but on occasion I'll see one in one of the bars. That's one of them you're playing, coincidentally."

I pointed to the initials 'ML' discretely etched on a lower corner.

"Well, I'll be," he said. "What does the 'ML' stand for?"

"Who cares?"

"Who cares indeed!" he laughed.

He walked over to the pill dispenser and came back with a large pill in his hand. He took it and went to the bar for a glass of water.

Coming back he explained: "Hydrocodone for the lithium headache later. I guess I've been here about an hour. Think I'll go sit on a bench and feed songbirds. I worked hard in the garden yesterday, so I'm happy to have a play day full of light feeling. Oh, by the way, they have cocoa leaves at the garden and hope to get a lot of work done if you're interested."

I said indeedie I was, and we both laughed. Most of us here still have a decent dose of work ethic, and if we can do some productive work now and again, we feel we're in a small part paying our way. And working after chewing cocoa leaves is like sailing on open water on a sunny day. Much better than using power tools, even if we had them.

We exchanged farewells and he slipped out the door. I slid over to the bar. The acting bartender asked what I would like.

"A cool thirty year old brunette, neat."

He grinned.

"Me too. I do have a cold three month old grape soda, canned. Or I could fix a short laudanum if it's not too early for you." Laudanum was the only way you could get alcohol here. The opium cured the craziness of booze, but it also puts you in a somber slumber.

"Grape's fine," I smiled.

I looked around at the happy faces of the tavern and thought: this is so finely weird.

The town garden was easy to find. All gardens are one block off the main drag, and the smell of freshly watered soil can pretty well lead the way. This one appeared to be a couple of acres or so, with a four-foot chain link fence around it to keep out the less-determined critters. There was a sadly overweight fellow sitting by the gate holding a basket of bright green leaves. His nametag read "Fleet."

I asked him what kind of work we were doing today.

He glanced at my nametag in return and replied that weeding and pruning were today's projects. "You need to be careful of the plant roots while weeding and be sure that they stay covered."

I asked if I could chew on some of the cocoa leaves.

"Four," he said. "Any more than that and we won't be able to chase you out of here till morning."

He handed me four small leaves and watched me place them in my mouth. Cocoa leaves can cause problems if used recreationally, so there is some oversight required.

"Thanks, Fleet."

Before I reached the first row of tomatoes, I felt cool wind in my sails and an undeniable desire to pluck weeds, even the tiny ones, from around each plant. I took inventory of my readiness for the job. No knee pads, no gloves, and no hat. Just a thousand tiny pulling jobs waiting to be done. What the heck. Busy time.

It's hard to explain the energy to work those leaves provide. It's not exactly a high, but it's an urgency to accomplish. I got on my hands and knees and began pulling weeds down a long row of tomatoes. I passed a couple of other folks that seemed to be focused on pinching suckers and planting them in little egg crates, so there was a minimum of small talk. It just felt good to be working on something so important. My goal here is to do one important thing a day. If I do two or three, I start thinking 'vacation!'

I attacked the weeds with a strange mix of care and abandon. Some of the larger weeds required more attention, as I believe that a good weeding job must include a solid majority of the roots. I let the victims lay where they fell, like the aftermath of some crazed gunslinger's spree.

After three long rows and about three hours, the weeds did not look so menacing, so I went and got a rake, collected the bodies, and deposited them in the compost bin. I was feeling pretty tired at this point. I checked out at the scanner, looked at my filthy clothes, and walked back to the main street to find a laundry.

The best thing about the laundries here is that they clean while you wait, and showers are available. The guy behind the counter frowned a bit when he saw how filthy my clothes were, but if they don't get clean they just give me new stuff.

There were several guys in the communal shower, some had been in the garden with me and some didn't have much dirt on. I love the dialogue in these places when being a little crowded:

"Don't pee on my leg and tell me it's raining. HEY, I SAID DON'T PEE ON MY LEG!"

"Another thing I don't like here is that you have to do everything by hand… including sex!"

"Can we get some more steam in here? Looking at all you guys is pretty depressing."

It was like turning the clock back to junior high school after football practice.

New clothes were waiting when I left the shower; evidently I had worn out the others. I'm sure it's all in the scan info, but I doubt anyone worries about another pair of wool trousers more or less.

One scan at the door and I was out into my busy, marvelous day.

A place like Opium Island wasn't needed years ago at the time social security was introduced. Then a person retired at sixty, had a few good years without having to worry about starving or being homeless thanks to that monthly check, and then died five years later after some good fishing trips with the grandkids. People over seventy were rare. Now medicine keeps everyone alive for so long that people over ninety are all over the place. And America isn't really for the oldsters, no matter how much Madison Avenue tries to project otherwise. Life is for the young and robust. Always has been. But all is not lost for the aged. We've been given a swell resort for the rest of our lives with no devices our grandchildren have to show us how to work. We are home with our generation, sharing, caring and occasionally daring. And if there's any melancholy to this state of affairs, it can be quietly subdued with the rose-colored glasses of pharmaceuticals.

As I walked toward the opium den I wondered what was done with all the scans. Obviously they were all collected in order to keep up with where we are and what we do. But do we have some sort of permanent record that they tie into as well?

Probably we each have a file that contains complaints by and against us, but is there a value system towards our other daily activities? I try to be helpful during the day and have little use for shenanigans. There's got to be another set of rules here, deeper that the obvious ones we circulate. There may even be secret rules against bringing these things up in conversation. But as far as I know, thinking them must be safe. This is no Kafka novel, best I can tell.

I stopped in at a taco stand and had three tacos. Sometimes when I do opium I forget to eat afterwards. I took two puffs from my thc wax pipe and before it could hit me I turned toward the inviting den vestibule.

The den was about half full as I walked in. I saw some familiar faces and nodded and grinned, getting the same in return. There was very little conversation, which was not unusual. Talking can't make you feel any better and can lead to petty conflicts. There was a chunk burning under an inverted glass bowl and I took a straw from the counter and slipped it into the space between the bottom edge of the bowl and the counter, getting a steady sip of the grey smoke. I held it lightly and turned it loose. The second sip was a little bigger, and I was able to caress it in my lungs a little longer. As the wispy exhalation floated toward the ceiling, I felt the pleasant sensation of loosing fifty pounds while my clothes kissed my skin.

I smiled largely at the beautiful people sitting around me, and took one more sip, which I held warmly inside for what seemed like an hour or so. Opening my eyes, I saw a very soft world that beckoned me to sun. I gently skated to the door and after scanning stretched out my arms, visually taking an inventory of all the things that appeared to be within my grasp. Just inside my shining right hand I saw a swing set only half occupied. I smoothly covered the intervening space and set in the rounded rubber seat. A weightlifter style belt was attached to the chains, so I snapped it snugly around my waist. It felt like a hug from the swing and my smile grew accordingly. As I kicked my feet forward and back encouraging the arc, I fully entered that world of participatory wonder and awe of feeling fully interactive with the world, as if it were finally sharing its deepest secrets. I flew out and fell back again and again feeling that I must soon die as I had just uncovered the final and ultimate meaning of existence. I felt so wise having smoked the thc wax first.

All too soon I felt a sorness in my knees. Although not painful, it was an obvious sign that it was time to change activities. I slowly came back to earth with light backward dragging of my shoes. I stood and started to walk away before noticing I was still tethered by the belt. I laughed, thinking I wasn't no damn genius after all.

I scanned at the railing leaving the set area, and just started walking towards the edge of town an inch or two above the pavement.

At the end of what serves as the main street is the residential area. First are the barracks for travelers and folks that like a more independent lifestyle. Next are duplexes where friends can maintain a family like closeness. Next are single homes for those who like to putter around the place. All of them are kept clean and comfortable by the residents; grubby folks who mess things up seem to not be around for too long. No doubt they are dealt with by those who live beyond the single homes in a rather cold-looking apartment style habitat: the nurses. I stopped in front of the barracks but decided it was too early to call it a day. There was some sun left and I was feeling high and good about myself from having worked today. So I walked back into the town proper.

I noticed a clinic with an open-air area between it and the beach. I stepped inside to see if someone wanted to go out into the sun. A fellow waved at me from his cot and I went and looked at his chart. 'Shake' was his nametag moniker which matched the name on the chart. It looked like an hour or so of sun would be ok. I looked at his face and it looked familiar.

"Hello, Glendale," he said without looking at my nametag.

"Hi, Shake. Would you like to go outside? There's some sun and it's sixty eight degrees."

There is a thermometer at each clinic doorway.

"Love to," he replied.

It was a simple matter to roll his cot out to the front courtyard abutting the main street sidewalk. I asked if he wanted to get up into a chair and he declined.

"I get a little dizzy sitting up sometimes," he said.

I asked if he wanted to hit my hash pipe.

"Sure, as long as I may be dizzy anyway."

He held the hit for a while then looked at the sky.

"This is a great place to be well or sick," he said.

I used a small handkerchief to wipe the pipe stem, and took a toke for myself.

I asked what he was in for.

"Slight stroke, they said. Left side's pretty weak. Just a watch and see situation for a few days. Been inside for two days. Thanks for coming by."

I asked how we knew each other.

"You passed through a couple of weeks ago and we played darts and talked at the opium den."

We use darts with plastic tips.

"I just remembered your face. Pretty good for a guy that's had a stroke, I guess," he offered.

"Indeed. Thanks for remembering. What did we talk about?"

"Well, we actually talked about why we came over here. I know that's kinda taboo, but, hell, we were high. I remember telling you I just got tired of visiting with my family who only looked at their telephones the whole time I was there, even at dinner. And it got boring watching other people play sports while I just sat in a chair, happy or sad based on the whims of the game. I wanted a primary life instead of a secondary one. And I got tired of everything having to be either good or bad when it really wasn't important enough to waste the judgment on. I guess I just got sick and tired of being sick and tired."

I didn't completely get that last part, but I nodded anyway.

I asked him what I said made me decide to end up here. I'm a little inconsistent with my stories sometimes, and I had no idea what I had told him.

"You said that the great white way had become too difficult with your failing memory. You said one of the real advantages to growing older here is you really don't need short term memory. You are where you are and there's no schedule to be anywhere else. Back in the previous life you were getting to be a bit of a bother to those around you by not remembering stuff. You said here it's ok; if you forget to eat, you're dieting. With all the pot around, that doesn't happen much though. I thought that was pretty funny."

I was glad I had told him that version. The truth is a little rough for me still, and I dislike exposing that self. I can't help but think back to the old days and some of the things I might have handled better. Just signing up and leaving without telling anyone was hard, but it would have been hard on someone however it was done. I could have talked it over with her first, let her know what I was going to do, but she just would have made me feel bad for running out on her. I didn't need that as my last memory of her. She wasn't going to leave her friends and beloved digital society to go to some sort of hippy resort for the rest of time. There the addiction was the emotional static of everyone's broadband relationships carried around in one's pocket. All that flurry of information with so little actually happening was just downright creepy to me. Besides, she was anti-drug while I have always been willing to let them say their piece. And here I can really hope for a human reunion with her if and when. Bottom line, I just thought a slower life was a natural oldster's lot. And it doesn't matter if what you think is true or not, it just needs to make you take action. And if everyone else wants to remain among the gizmos, so be it. In fact, family in its best and highest purpose provides for oldsters and always has. I'm just not sure we feel we have time to act our best.

Thinking back, in that world I was generally frustrated; my desires were trumped by outside whims. I was probably typical of the many people who find themselves giving in to more social personalities. On Opium Island my own decisions work out just fine. I don't think that coming here was a harmful decision; I just chose a complete change. And regardless of what inertia promised, a drastic change of some sort was going to be my lot at some point. This way I contributed the element of choice, to make myself the only responsible agent of my current state. Anyway, that's the way things ended and began, for worse or for better. Rationalizing I know, but I wasn't very connected there; here either, I suppose. But it doesn't hurt here.

Now I feel like getting on with my job of getting high… Pot takes me back there sometimes, but it's usually my friend.

"You deep in thought or just stoned?"
I smiled and said sometimes it's easier to let the pot do my thinking.
"But thinking is all pot can fix," he said, then continued:
"We are ruled by the resistance to being ruled by physics. We wish to wish. Every day I wake up hoping to find I've changed into my next stage, some beautiful butterfly. But always a failure to morph. The promise of dope always remains just a promise."
I suggested he aim a little lower.

"Start with moth. Move up to butterfly."
He grinned.
Thanks for the laugh, he said.
I asked him if he wanted me to take him back inside or leave him out. That it was time for my boot-heels and all that.
"Oh, just leave me here. There'll be a Samaritan coming by before too long. Unless a nurse comes and gets me for getting into some taboo talk."
Sometimes we mentioned nurses like they were bogeymen; deep inside we did have a healthy respect for them. I said I'm sure he would be all right, and wished him luck.

I can't tell you too much about the nurses because I don't know too much. Nobody does, probably including the nurses. It's all an experiment with a bunch of old doomed volunteers who have signed their lives away. They have to enforce some kind of order, to deal with troublemakers; knowing they will never be second-guessed may make it harder rather than easier, if such is the case. I hope it's a beneficent organization with lots of individual warnings before anything too drastic is done and that seems to be the case. I do see fewer and fewer really rude folks here, and if that's a priority with them that's ok with me. But in any case, even though we hardly ever see them, they have all the say so. And we're obviously very easy to kill.

Just then two nurses in their blue and white striped skirts and blue bonnets came out of the building. They smiled and began to roll Shake back into the clinic. I noticed that one of the nurses seemed to have a little chin stubble. That did not surprise me, of course, as it's pretty clear that all nurses are dressed like ladies, being one or not. I guess it's to give a more motherly feeling to this society, with an atmosphere of 'we'll take care of that.' It also promotes a more genteel attitude toward them and each other, which is the basis of this little society. It's not a 'be nice or leave' requirement, but more of an 'I wonder what happened to that rude guy?' Survival of the best fits.

One thing that I have learned over here that seems to be some late character growth is that you can always do the right thing. We're all old enough to generally know what the right thing to do is in most situations, and we should do that thing regardless. The corollary to that is that you can never make someone else do the right thing. If you say 'good morning' to the same person every day for a month when you see him on a walk, that's generally the right, and nice, thing to do. If he never says 'good morning' back, you would be tempted to stop saying anything, but you continue saying 'good morning' not because you get a response that feels good, but because it is the right thing for you to do. In the old world I often determined my relationships based on how that other person treated me. If they were cool, I was cool. If they were friendly, then was I. That required the making of assumptions, which we humans are not always the best at. I have found that it is much easier and consistent to treat everyone as if they were being nice to me, regardless of if they are or not. After all, we're all in hospice here; were back in the old world too, just didn't want to admit it. Besides, over here if someone ignores what you say, there's a fifty-fifty chance he or she is just deaf.

I wish I had figured that out back in the great white way, but I was usually feeling a little rattled and insecure back there. For that reason I rarely think back before the choice. I know there were pros and cons about coming over here. But in the final analysis leaving there and coming here just seem like the right thing to do. And when I passed my physical it was like mother nature had given her blessing to the crossing. I think choosing the new name I got over here helped quite a bit because there was no pressure to have even been somebody before here. I was who I was now and not because of any old baggage, no matter how nice or bad it might have been. As long as I just focus on the high, I surpass myself here. I have direction. Up.

And the great white way seemed to be rushing

headlong and at increasing velocity towards something, and in my mind there was a great uncertainty towards what. It's like building a train track faster and better every day while the destination of that track becomes lost in a haze of successful track building. Growing up under the nuclear attack dog, is annihilation the only end we can see? Will there be inflation, where there are a lot of things wanted but few can afford, or will there be deflation, with many distractions available but little interest in them. And suppose we reach the social nirvana of looking at others and truly seeing ourselves, what then? Will our heads explode because we reached the peak of homo sapianism? I am sure that in the largest possible picture, the universe is guiding us, but we seem unable to catch its wind in our sails. Maybe the sail is our map, but looking understandingly at each other is not going to raise or read it. We need to reinvent ourselves as new searchers for truth. We need common frontiers. We all need to recapture the wonder of what is over, under, around and out there. By stepping back from track building, perhaps we can envision an inclusive future for all, in a world of human stewardship over human domination. Not all things to all people, but all people open to all good things. Some sort of quantum religion that is there but lets us be there as well.

Wow! That last hit at the clinic was a good one!

I didn't use drugs much in the old world, but I've acclimated well. Heck, I've darn near baby duck imprinted on the stuff.

In the old days, I would have gone into a bar on a day like this and had a beer or few. But no beer, or any alcohol much, is part of this new world. In the old world, humanity had come to an accommodation with alcohol: alcohol won. Here we let cooler heads prevail; opium lets that happen. But you can't let opium sit on you; you have to keep moving and feeling and seeing and helping. Opium can help unfreeze you. Opium lets one sit back from one's self. It's like taking a chair about four feet back and just watch that entity called 'me' going on. I watch myself run into problems, make decisions, good and bad, have fun and get depressed. All without judging too harshly. Have you ever had your life pass in front of your eyes? You don't judge what you've done; you just marvel in all the things that were you. So my philosophy is to get up, get dressed, get busy, see what happens and then go on, letting others do any judging if they have the time and inclination. There's just the done and undone, and the mind works more happily moving ahead. And when you participate rather than just watch, even to some limited degree, the whole world comes alive and celebrates in its appreciation of you. And at the end, maybe the universe will give you a little hug.

The sun was getting low, so I headed for the lazy lodge to find a bed and chill for the evening. I scanned as I went in and saw a lot of empty beds. I went over to the linens shelf and picked out a set and went back to make up a cot. Afterwards, I walked to the buffet and made a ham sandwich, took it outside and set at a small table with two other gents after asking if I might join them. I started to question my decision to sit here when I heard the two discussing the old world.

"Yeah, I've heard about our folks being 'the best generation,' but I can't see it that way," a skinny guy with a beret said with a sour look on his face.

"Seems to me they were about the worst generation. They got in late in the bloodiest war in history, let the Russians do most of the dirty work, clear cut soldier and civilian, friend and foe with a million bombs, and then come home with all the spoils of war and the only super-sized economy. They ran the commercial world with a big stick to end up owning about ninety percent of everything worth anything on this planet, willing to share only if they got concessions to get more stuff. No sir, that's not great.

And what about us, their kids? Wanted us to have everything money could buy. But they had no desire for companion time, no leadership or instruction. No educational or moral apprenticeship. Get outta this house and go to school and find a pseudo family your own age. All the time justifying pushing us away for being long haired, dope smoking, devil-music lovers, so they could pursue their real interest of 'my way or the highway.' Power and money. They sure had it. And the worst thing they did was to pass that morality on to us. "

I just slightly nodded. Talk gets like this sometimes when there's more thc in the system than pain relief. It sure doesn't make you homesick for the great white way he's trashing. He looked at me for a spell.

"Do you even have a clue as to what was happening?"

"Clue maybe. Not an answer to all that, no."

I excused myself after finishing my sandwich, and went back inside. That kind of talk is pretty gritty for a place where the past is best left alone. America's past and its future are not of this island. We don't get news about anything for a reason. Even though we may not know exactly why, one thing is clear. Don't go there. We don't much, and it's pretty obvious there are microphones just about everywhere. Old trash talk can create an unwelcome uneasiness here. I go in thinking I may see that beret down the trail someday without a person underneath it.

Inside the barracks there's a large screen on the back wall with a movie with lots of birds in it. They are pretty and graceful. They look like the same birds I marveled at as a child, but were in reality probably those birds great-great-great-great-great grandchildren. I finish my sandwich and go back to my bed. Which one was it? Dang. I usually leave my toothbrush on the pillow to help me remember, but didn't this time. I chose one and took off my clothes and settled in. Que sera. After thirty minutes of tossing I went to the bathroom, scanned the dope machine, punched the xanax button twice and downed them with a glass of water. I went back to my bed and spun softly into morning.

Lying in bed with the sun lightly shining through, I lounged. I enjoy sitting back and thinking about things some mornings, before drugs and events start taking over. I like to think about this place, and how I feel so summer free here. Not middle of the summer free when the prospect of school begins to loom, but the first day of summer free when all is possible and wonderful and the horizon is one step away! I think about how this place must have been set up, and like to think it was constructed on practical considerations, and not just 'let's be nice to the old folks' kind of public program or a subtlely more sinister 'let's get rid of the old folks' pogrom.' I sometimes think this whole thing could have been set up to save money. Pensions, either government or private, must have been getting too expensive. Medical care for the elderly a hundred times more so. And it's not like we're wanted after sixty anyway. We refused to retire and let young folk have jobs, we squeeze savings till green ink runs like turnip blood, and we insist democratically on a society that caters to us because we have a lot of what it takes to get along as well as the jobs and the government.

This place is cheap to run. It's low-tech analogue where the great white way is high-tech digital. No phones, no cars, no factories, no calendars. No money. No credit. Just living and dying in a place some of us decided would be comfortable, with the chance of feeling productive now and then. And there's also the feeling of doing the right thing, of getting out of the gal dern way so youth can forge ahead. People only kept on decrepitly living because medicine made it that way, and the only reason medicine made the decision that too-long lives were good is because that decision made it so much money. If all old people were poor, being over sixty-three would be a rarity. So without the hypocrisy, I can feel like life here is perfect for me. Perfect. Perfect. One life: one chance at feeling perfect.

I finally rose as the sunshine retreated toward the half opened doorway. I grabbed my sheets and pillowcase and walked back to the laundry behind the sleeping area. No one was manning the machines, so I figured I would start the day with a little public service. I gathered up the pile of sheets that had been abandoned by the early risers, and placed them loosely in the commercial-sized washer. I filled the laundry cup once with detergent and poured it over the wash. Everything here that has to be measured is always one cup. It's not that we're idiots here; but there are a few, and when a large percentage of the community is high and or senile, it's best to keep things in the low numbers.

As the washer ran I walked over to the breakfast bar and turned on the skillet to make a couple of eggs. They fried pretty quickly and were ready when the skillet automatically shut off. I placed them between two slices of bread and walked over to the washer. Near the wall I saw a pill dispenser and sauntered over to see if anything looked appropriate for the day. After running down the usual list, I decided to forgo and make this a library day. I can read high actually, but I get kinda bored doing the same page over and over.

I enjoyed my egg sandwich standing alongside the washer and watching it spin.

When the washer stopped running I transferred the load to the dryer and pressed the button that said dry. I was tempted to leave, but decided to wait for the folding part, as that is the toughest part of a pretty easy job. I gave a big old come hither arm swing when the done bell rang on the dryer and one of the lazybones who had just gotten up came over and we folded each item together. We folded them pretty well for a couple of geezers, and placed them on the rack where we had picked them up the day before. Good work, I thought. Time to relax with a good book.

I walked over to the library located next door and mystifyingly close to the opium den. I resisted a sudden impulse to change my plan, and slid on into the land-o-books. There were volumes and volumes of books on shelves that reached no higher than the average old guy could reach easily without the aid of a stool or ladder. All the books were older than the initial date of the island, just to make double sure the ban on outside news was strictly observed. The lack of news here is difficult at first, because literally all folks have to talk about is the weather. We hear nothing about the outside world except from the new arrivals, and they are so scared of getting into Dutch spreading rumors that they say very little. Wars, plagues, hurricanes all happen without our ever knowing. Not that we really care after awhile. It was all mostly news about things we could do nothing about, presented by a media that was pawning off ads to a nervous clientele that shopped for the stuff to feel like they did have some control in life. No shopping on the island; hence no need to jive us up. So our ignorance here is exceeded only by our apathy.

There was also a table of comic books that seem to have been gone through often. A fella would have to be extra high not to enjoy a good comic, with a complete adventure in eight pages. Looking back at the bookshelf, I began to peruse the titles available. Lots of crime dramas and history. Lots of art. I pulled down a coffee table sized book of modern art and turned a couple of pages. I could look at pictures by Klee and Kandinsky all day long. They have a certain affirmative feel, much the same as pictures done by children. I'll bet their mothers put their paintings on their refrigerator doors long after they were grown. It inspired me to go find an activity center where I could do some drawing. Conveniently, the arts activity studio was nearby.

I scanned in at the door and found some art supplies on the back wall of the studio.

Lifting a large sheet of art paper and a dark pencil, I found an empty table and sat down to see what inspiration might come. Strangely, high my creativity is not very good, and though it's fun to move colors around in that state, the finished product is a trash heap someone threw a rainbow on.

I began making circles, drew a large one and put a small face at the bottom of it. I began to draw images in the massive skull, first a car, then a phone, then some folding money and coins, then a calendar, then a stoplight, and finally a group of children. That pretty much filled the circle. To that I added a diagonal line, to make the European none-of-that-here sign. I pondered life without all those items and their propensity to make one anxious or nervous, but maybe most of all self-conscious and a little inferior feeling. I returned to the face at the bottom of the page supporting the huge skull-o-stuff, and added a smile. Art with an insight. Sometimes even without psychic enhancement I feel like I might be part genius.

And speaking of irritations, one would be the mix of oldsters and automobiles. Saying our driving's ok because of our wealth of highway experience is like saying a fifty year old linebacker has made a lot of tackles so he could still well serve the Packers. Look out convenience store wall; the accelerator is starting to feel a lot like the breaks!

We don't feel much road rage, but we do cause it. And heaven help the world when we're backing up. Old person and car have gone far enough. So none here.

No one really misses them one bit. And though the mortality rate is high here, it's not because of drive by shootings.

Making such dramatic comment on our state of the world led me to take a little pipe puff and ponder just how free we are here from those irritating things. I felt the thc starting to stir so I sat back in my chair and looked out the window as if my thoughts were about to get so big the large studio couldn't contain them. So free, so free. So free to…? The freedom here also leads to sense of longing for some ultimate. Of course when I say freedom, I mean freedom and dope. Here we live the animal, with the satisfaction of food and shelter. And we live the social, choosing just how much society we want at a certain time. Perhaps that should be enough, to interact with others and exchange empathies. But, probably because when you're high you always want to get higher, we want to find some ultimate truth above animal and social obligations and rewards. Some condition where we can look down from a fair distance at the animal and social things we do as interesting components of the real us that exists beyond inside and out; where no one is second to anyone or anything else, now or in the history of life on earth. That would be a nice detached place in the company of amoebas, dinosaurs and mockingbirds. It would probably come with a fireplace, sweater and a pipe full of sweet tobacco. And heck, while I'm at it, let's throw in an easy chair and a picture on the side table of a smiling most-beautiful-girl-in-the-world.

I may not have that all figured out today, but I'm happy because I will probably figure it out tomorrow.

All that being said, it just seemed like a good day to enhance with a quay. Sunshine begetting sunshinier.

I walked to the dispenser and hit a quay button and watched it fall into the crucible. I downed it with a full cup of water. I smiled and took the first step into what would be the day's offering. I took out my pipe and had a nice hit of thc just to see what sort of adventure might be found. I started to stroll at a confident canter. Something just felt pretty right.

I saw the coffee shop sign ahead and almost without thinking turned in the door. I love the beatnik clubs. Having coffee high and listening to poetry or singing for an hour or two just keeps a grin on my face. I can't finger snap my applause as well as some because of the arthritis in my hands. The dress code is loosened a bit in here and you can wear a beret and thick black glasses. Strangely, melancholy music is not popular, mostly by public's disenchantment with focusing on the past; we want to hear about today and tomorrow.

I scanned the room a saw a couple of ladies together at a small table near the bar. A couple of geezers were trying to make headway from a table nearby, but it was pretty obvious their bullshit was DOA. I passed closer on my way to the counter to get a hot chocolate, and one of the pretty biddies gave me a short glance. I looked them over at close range and saw two attractive ladies with nametags at admirable slants. What the heck? No reason to be fearful of trying.

"Would you enchanting ladies be so kind as to watch my drink while I humbly enlighten and entertain from the stage?"

They exchanged a short glance and the one who espied me earlier responded in the affirmative with a slight nod and slighter grin.

I pulled out my pipe and casually placed it by my cup.

"Lest I be tempted to take a second toke of this marvelous wax. But please, ladies, if you wish…"

I stepped up onto the small stage at the side of the room. I scanned the audience as they began to quieten, noticing my stance behind the mike.

There were about fifteen people in the bar, with five of them being ladies, an almost unheard of percentage of fems. I quickly made friends with the butterflies in my stomach and put my left hand on the microphone pole.

"Hello friends! On this lovely day punctuated by a plethora of lovely ladies, I humbly beseech you the favor of your attention for the reciting of some poetry composed and performed by your unworthy servant for your entertainment."

The quay and pot were starting to dance between my ears and my eyes were beholding the warm glow of brotherhood, giving me a stageborn permission of go-ahead.

I looked to the low ceiling and began a poem I made up a few days ago in the opium room:

"I wonder where we'll go from here
If Opium Island disappears.
Is there another place for us?
Or shall we only find we're dust?
It doesn't matter what we face;
Dead or alive we'll whiz through space!"

"Can you be a little more depressing?" came a shout from the left side of the room.

I looked at the table where I had left my drink and noticed the two ladies there were puzzling lightly. I flushed, but quickly regained my smile. "My apologies for such a clumsy effort! If I may be permitted a lighter note..."

Without waiting for a reply I began, while looking where my distracter had sounded:

"Brighten up my chickadee
And see the things that you can be.
Lover, confidant and friend
Always backed by life's cool wind.
All we know is change is certain.
Jump on the stage and raise the curtain.
You may just surprise yourself
And find you are on life's top shelf!
From way up here you may espy
Just why it is we live so high!"

At that there was a general light round of applause which I modestly absorbed and stepped down from the stage. I walked back to my cup of chocolate and the lady that had smiled at me earlier indicated a chair at the table. I said thank you and sat. My mind was still flush with the pleasurable push of the pill, so I pressed my luck.

"On a night like this, ladies, the call of romance is almost deafening. It must either be ignored or enhanced! I suggest we retire to a cozy cubicle in nearby music store and throw the cushions on the floor!"

The girls gave me a pretty good look then looked at each other. The girl of perpetual quiet asked: "Quays, right?"

Staring lovingly in her eyes, I responded: "Indeed!"

Then slight grin continued: "Do you have a friend?"

"Ladies, ladies! This is love's invitation, not a negotiation!"

Again they looked at each other.

"Let's quay up," said the girl of perpetual quiet.

Slight grin grinned.

As the girls sauntered over to the pill dispenser, I rushed to the men's room and quickly removed my plastic undies, putting them in my back pocket. I figured my reasoning in doing this was pretty sound with my prospects for girling so solid.

And I felt absolutely guilt free, as my legal marriage in the old world had been trumped by my being legally dead there. Death did us part.

As I got back to the table, I saw the ladies returning from the ladies, and asked them if they wanted another toke as the grip of shyness began to loosen.

"Sorry, I can't hear you… The call of romance is too deafening!" said little grin smiling largely.

"Let's go listen to some music!"

All I can really say about the rest of the evening is it was the song of the three commandoes.

Maturity.

Know-how.

Savoir-faire.

A little creek of pleasure that flowed into the river of joy that fell face first into the sea of ecstasy…

The sun was in my eyes and I woke slowly.
Alone. A little heart was painted in lipstick
around my navel. Two would have been nice.
Que era, era. I grinned and noticed my face was
sore. I must have been doing a lot of smiling.
I was beat. The humour was off me now. I
started to get dressed. I grabbed a shoe and
reminded myself 'toes first.'
I felt a little funky, and rather than chance
running into the girls again while not bolstered
by the quays, I decided to let motion be my
guide and take the train to still new adventures.
I already had my toothbrush, so there was no
packing to do. I walked to the train station and
scanned, then turned to the nearest passenger
car and stepped aboard.
"Au revoir," I said aloud to the beautiful village
of Bea.

I wasn't sure what the next town would be like,
or even if I had ever been there before. It didn't
matter. I just enjoyed the eight miles per hour
shuttle down the tracks.
Finally another passenger came in and sat down
on the other side of the car. He had a nametag, of
course, but sometimes I don't even bother to
read them. I said hello and he nodded.
"Do you know the name of the next town?" he
inquired.
"No, I'm afraid I don't."
I wasn't actually afraid, but it did come out that
way.

"I probably should go ahead and walk; it would do me good to exercise," he said, then added, "What the heck," and walked over to the pill case in front of the car. He scanned, pushed a button, and two pills fell out into his hand. He took them with a cup of water from the water fountain at the front of the car. I don't know what pills they were, but he was very quiet all the way through the trip.

The train ride gave me an opportunity to inventory. This would have been impossible in the old world; I had too much stuff. I imagine that even folks back there that think they don't have a lot of stuff actually do when it comes down to enumerating. Probably at least a hundred things I suppose. I had many more: books, records, photos, letters. Stuff people keep in common on digital devices now. Then there were toiletries, clothes, cars, cooking things. Lots to keep up with. I did my inventory quickly: shirt, pants, jacket, shoes, socks, funky underwear, pipe, pot and a toothbrush. Then I turned my palm up and looked at my barcode: there is most of my stuff, I thought, and I don't even know where or what all it is.

The train pulled into the station just as the sun was rising. Trains rarely arrived after dark; it would probably be too disorienting for a lot of us. The sign over the depot door said

'Baileytown.' I grinned. How richly ironic. I didn't even know where to twisted think first. So I grabbed my pipe and took a deep draught of waxen fog.

Crossing over to the registration desk and being scanned, I noticed a nurse guiding a gent by the elbow towards me.

"Would you mind showing this gentleman around?" the nurse asked.

"Not at all. Hello. My name's Glendale."

"Hi, Glendale. I appreciate it." The man's nametag said 'Tank.'

I noted that seemed like a strange moniker to select for his new rest of his life name.

"I was always small. Never got to be the big guy even in my own imagination. So when they said pick a name, I jumped at Tank. I could have gone Zeus, I guess, but that would be a little showy."

I laughed.

The nurse retreated toward the medical door at the back of the depot. I had been asked to show folks around before, as the nurse well knew. I was not going to ever say no to a nurse. Bad for the health to, it was generally assumed.

"Is this your first day here?"

"Second. I just went through registration and got some general information. I just don't want to screw up. They made it sound pretty rough if you do, although they didn't go into much detail about what screwing up consisted of."

He gave me a slightly concerned look.

"Well, you just don't want to cause trouble," I cautioned him. "Even for those of us who have been here for a while, we don't know if the straight and narrow is a tightrope or a four lane highway. But mostly it's a great place if you stay outta other folks' business. Be helpful and work at the businesses here. It's easy stuff mostly and others tend to stay out of your face. As long as you're being helpful or high all is well. The pecking order is already well established here: nurses then everybody else. You can be stupid here, but probably not for long."

He looked a little dejected.

"I hope I made the right decision coming here."

I suggested he not think of it as a decision.

"It's your new life. You are now legally dead to the old one. There's a funeral after you leave there, you know, and all contact with that world is over forever. Some folks just have to know what's going on back home, so the nurses will provide an update session, where they will tell you that your loved ones are doing great and have built a little shrine in your memory. All a crock, but I guess it lets some folks sleep better. And even if those left behind could contact you over here, it would probably just be to ask where you put the other set of keys to the Buick. So the less you think about the past and even having made a decision, the better off you'll be. Heck, it's great here! I promise you won't hurt here unless you really want to."

We walked out onto the main street.

"Look at all the stuff to do! There's a little café where you can get some breakfast. A little further is an opium pub. And though it looks unmanned now, a hot dog stand on the beach. Maybe you'll get it opened today. Benches in the sun. Brooms to sweep the lawns here and there. Looks like a full fun day to me. We don't focus on what we've lost; we focus on what we have." He smiled.

"I don't really care for these plastic lined underpants we have to wear here, though," he said sheepishly.

I laughed.

"You'll get used to them. A pair may even be your best friend some day."

I thought back to the day I arrived here. That's as far back as I like to go. I remember the great white way as a place that relished the technological advances that pushed the slower elderly more and more out of the light and onto the tracks.

There was no statue of liberty waiting for us here either. But it wasn't bad at all. It was old folks checking in the new old arrivals and the welcome was with smiles: 'with opium arms.' There was the sound of the surf and the ancient majesty of the pelican, a bird that seems to have made an easy transition from dinosaur. I got my first tattoo, a bar code traced onto my right palm. And I saw my first surveillance camera, the first of thousands. But that was ok, too. They were made to look more like bar lights than gun barrels.

"Not many women here," he said.
"Not many women here and they get harassed for sex by a lot of goobers but they really like it because without any competition from the seventeen to sixty four set, they get all the attention and pampering. And they look great as a lot of them will spend their soon to be useless money on body remodeling. Also, the nurses are good about making sure a dog doesn't get a free bite, so things rarely get out of hand. With no alcohol or guns here, and just limited amounts of testosterone, crimes of passion are a rarity."
"I haven't seen any churches here yet either."
"They are here but usually a street back or so. Religion here is really pretty free flowing. Bible thumpers don't seem to come here much in the first place, because of the permissiveness. If they do and get too in your face, the nurses usually take care of them with a little slap on the holy spirit.
The real opiate of the masses here is opium. We choose to be docile under the influence. And be as productive as we can under our limitations, all without a lot of pressure of sticks or carrots. We all know we're going to die here, become saints of the soil, and that's ok. I figure that all new life has to come from those that have lived

before. All that decayed stuff works its way towards the sun, getting filtered through dna to become a tree, a cricket, or my aunt Suzie. A great ballet really. One that we can dance, but we can't change. In the old life, people thought they could, but they were just fooling themselves."

"That was pretty deep," he said after a short pause.

"Pot talk is a lot different from chit chat or cocktail talk. As a matter of fact, some people will pot talk you to distraction if you let them. The safe word here is 'puppytalk.' If anything gets too hairy, just say 'puppytalk' and whatever is going on has to stop. No explanations, no hard feelings. It's just necessary in a place like this. It's nurse approved. They should have told you about that."

"They did, but it didn't mean anything. Now I see. 'Puppytalk.'"

I quieted and looked at him.

"Just kidding."

I smiled.

"Anything else you are curious about?"

He looked at his shoes.

I could tell he wasn't completely comfortable, and was trying to decide how to handle his insecurity.

"I guess not. I just need to find my way on my own. It's my adventure."

I smiled at him again.

"Atta boy! And don't worry, there are a lot of groups that have a lot of fun here; I'm just more of a loner. You can find a perfect life here if you are able to think a perfect life. And don't worry too much about the drug thing. It's pretty well understood that while scanning, the dispenser reads your blood dope level and will issue a placebo if you are too near the edge. ODs are rare. Barking at the moon not so much."

He grinned and said he'd go take a look at the shelter situation and see what might fit him best.

"I might see you around," he said.

"Fare you well," I replied.

I was tired at that point. Gravity now had the edge that the quay had last night. The quay giveth and the quayless taketh away. Only with a slight vengeance though. God bless the no hangover formula of life here.

I had a bite at the local barracks buffet and walked down to the opium den; always open. Two tokes seemed like plenty and I wobbled a mite as I searched for a quiet spot to recharge. I found a small trail that went back into the woods a ways, and sat on a bench under some beautiful fall trees. I sighed as I watched a symphony of leaves catching each breeze.

Everybody needs a favorite thing in life, and mine happens to be dancing leaves, falling so gracefully in the fall and at the mercy of the wind, its own shape determining its dance. It's like life itself from the limb to the loam, from the cradle to the grave. Green leaves spend their whole lives working from dawn to dusk, catching sun and turning it into chlorophyll or whatever for the greater good; while the tree grows, it gets worn out. But finally it starts to change from working class green to elite hues of red and orange, flinging itself into the eternity of what's-out-there to do the dance of the ever after. So beautiful, so complete, and in marvelous color. And there's also the cool and macabre dance of the dead, where already fallen leaves get caught by the wind and do their zombie-like swirls and loops with a zillion other dead leaves across roads and pathways. High or not I love this stuff.

As dusk approached, I got up to begin the walk back to the barracks. The little path had taken me to the more permanent residential part of town. Pleasantly walking down the sidewalk I noticed some wallflowers in small pots attached to the side of a duplex and felt they looked a little dry. I saw a dipper and well nearby, so I strolled over and remedied their thirst. As yardens took the place of flowers and grass here, it's nice to still have the flowers available in this way.
I put a little water in each of the pots and pinched off some spent blooms. I was going to throw them in the street, but thought better of it and placed them in a nearby compost can. I was

concerned about how the nurses might view littering, even of the organic variety.

I like to think I'm not obsessed with the nurses, but when you have to imagine what the rules may be, it keeps your civility on its toes. How big the box is of social behavior, I don't know. Is it growing or shrinking? Who knows? All I know is I have not made a fatal move thus far. Not even a warning. But are warnings even required? All I know to do is keep my nose clean, so to speak, and sincerely believe I am thriving here. Without money, position or family here, the only evidence of success is how you feel. And I usually feel pretty high.

I looked at the duplex's yarden and noted it was all lettuce. I appreciated the fact that here no one raises grass; watering and gardening effort here go to producing food for everyone to share.

I felt a little hunger pang and sauntered toward the sign that said 'Diner.' There was a short line in front of the restaurant. Looking through the window I saw the kitchen looked pretty empty, although the 'cook needed' sign was not out. I walked on through the green painted door and back to the kitchen and found no one at the stove. There were about a dozen or so people sitting at tables and about half that many more milling around, looking pretty stoned, and deciding if they were going to sit or go. The guy in front of the line had a nametag that said 'Wonderboy.' I asked him if he would like to help me cook some dinner. He said sure and we went back to the kitchen and checked the refrigerator. There were several bags of chicken parts and several jars of salsa.

I told the group that we're having Mexican chicken in about fifteen minutes.

As I turned on the grill to high and opened the chicken I told Wonderboy to check for chips or tortillas. With the grill hot I tossed on the chicken pieces and watched them sizzle. They were pretty, I thought; almost like reanimating the chicks for one final show. That gave me the idea of reaching for my pipe. Then I thought maybe I'd better not smoke before cooking and risk some zombie chicken experience.

The grill turned off as it does automatically after seven minutes. I turned it back on and flipped each of the twenty or so chicken pieces. I looked over at Wonderboy and he was staring into the cabinet. I reached under the Formica worktop and put a large saucepan on the grill. Into it I emptied three jars of salsa. I looked back at Wonderboy and he was still staring into the cabinet. I walked over, looked in and saw some large bags of tortilla chips.

"Let's use those," I said.

He said "Oh" and got two bags and brought them over to the counter.

"Get two dozen plates from the cabinet there and put a handful of chips on each one."
He began doing that and I watched the chicken pieces finish up. With a pair of tongs I took each piece of chicken and put on one per plate right in the middle of the small stack of chips. With a large spoon I ladled about a cup of salsa on each piece of chicken. I went back to the refrigerator and looked for cheese, but only found a block, none grated. Too late to add that now.
Wonderboy and I served the plates to the folks sitting around. Each diner said thanks and I replied that they were welcome.
I was thinking someone would volunteer to take the next shift of cooking as several people including Wonderboy and me were still unfed. But as no one did, I went back to the fridge and found some ground beef patties. I put some on the grill and turned it on. Wonderboy was sitting a table by himself looking out the window, so I went back to the cabinet and got a bag of bread slices and three cans of cut beans. I emptied the beans into the salsa pan thinking the little bit of salsa remaining would season the beans a little. After seven minutes the grill cut off. I turned the patties and restarted the grill. I got out some more plates. I went back to the fridge and found some brown gravy. I put the whole jar contents into a small pan on the grill and hoped it would be ready about the same time as the meat. As the grill cut off, I put a piece of bread on each plate, followed by a patty and then some gravy.

The salsa beans I put on the side. I served eight plates and took mine and Wonderboy's over to his table.

"Thanks," he said. "We survive on love and luck, don't we?"

I asked him what he meant.

He looked around the room as if it made everything clear. "Love is giving stuff, and luck is getting stuff."

I asked if that was the secret to life.

"No," said Wonderboy." The secret to life is having no secrets. Do what you do, good or bad, with your head held high, always confident in front of truth's ever-rolling camera."

Hmm.

I decided to walk down the street to the barracks and get some sleep. Seeing a couple of dudetts on the way, I smiled broadly in front of truth's ever-rolling camera.

I woke up with the feeble feeling that this was a Sunday. I walked outside before having breakfast and hit my pipe to do an early morning think.

The strangest thing about this place is we never know what time, or even what day, it is. Such temporal reality can be ignored or made up on an individual basis, I guess. Of course we know the cold season, and the summer, and when its time to plant when the seeds show up outside the gardens and the yardens. But it does give a curious floating feeling that there is just this day and we relive it over and over. Add this to the fact that new people show up now and then and old faces are not always quite remembered due to age and dope, and there's a feeling of wanting to make the most of, rather than just trying to get through, each day. And when things do get a little rutty, we can always just ride the train or stroll to another town with different attractions. While my mind is still on this topic, I have a nice hit of wax from my pipe. Soon I start thinking about how a dog might see each day, as the same but different because things are always happening. How there's a big guy, a food and water bowl, and a million smells to ponder. And how everything that that happens is normal. And how everything can be cured by licking it. And how important is to protect my relationship with the guy that fills the dishes. And what does that guy do with the poop he collects in little plastic bags? And then I started thinking about being that guy.

I thought of other creatures he kept, watched and fed. Pups and kittens. Chickens and pigs and cows. Snakes and birds. Zoo anythings. I guess all provide him with a feeling of power and dominance. Maybe we can't feel fully as human as we want to without those feelings. Once humanity is at a certain high level, our own weaknesses and disappointments seem at least of a higher domain than the rest of the animal kingdom. Of which we are the kings, I suppose.

And are we as old folks a little less than human now? Perhaps oldsters aren't really being kept. Suppose we are just being unkept and put out of the way as you would try to hide a painful embarrassment. In our prime, we may have taken too much; maybe their new society of constant communicating wants to create the present on sharing terms and without our selfish I me mine bigotry of possessions we felt so important.

Sometimes I see the seedy side that stems from smoking pot; thinking too deep sometimes leads to rapture, but sometimes just headaches.

I walk down to the opium den and find I'm the first one in. I have a puff, and start to feel a pang of worthlessness. Then the drug takes me out the door to this wonderful place; it's like a huge field with golden grasses waving in the wind. It is so wonderful because I can see so far, hear the rush of the wind, smell the crispness of fresh air, and feel the security of the sunshine bringing in constant good. So much like the vibrant, pulsating connection between the sun, moon, tides and heartbeats. It also reminds me of an epiphany long ago, when I felt all this fullness and knew how essential it was, and that the whole world was on the verge of a great understanding. So many years later now, but the understanding must still be out there, perhaps still willing to be found.

Almost as if to purposely mock that emotion, at that moment I saw two nurses, one on each side of an elderly gentleman who was sitting on a bench. The way they lifted him, he was obviously a goner, and from the way he was being carried it was obvious he was dead. They half-drug him to the nurses door at the rear of the barracks and then disappeared inside. No muss no fuss. How can death not even be a distraction?

It's so ironic. In the great white way, life for the elderly is pretty brutal and frustrating, both within and without, but society does every drastic thing it can to extend that life year after year after year. Here, life for the geezer and biddy is pretty good, but no effort is really made to give even an extra day. I guess by taking money out of the picture, us oldsters aren't so indispensable after all. That's a harsh thought and I wouldn't say it out loud, but really.
I felt a poem coming on:

There was no life of promise of good
So it was extended as long as it could.
And when things got good for leaving all sorrow
We find there's no effort made for tomorrow!

Opium may not be the best drug on the island,
but it sure helps you make things rhyme!

Melancholical pangs by now have settled in.

Today I'm wondering how life will end.
What will quench my desire?
Will there be mountains of fire
That someone I don't know will send?
What will lift us to that rest
And an end to all we possess?
When the race is run,
Replication done,
Let's fly off to the world of pretend!

I grin at myself. Pretty good for a
whippersnapper.

I see a barber shop just ahead, ha ha, and decide
on a cut. It's one more positive thing done in a
day and makes for casual visiting. I sometimes
think I would like to play barber, but of course
that is one of the jobs you actually have to have
some training in to work on people. I put my
jacket on the rack and have a seat under the wall
to wall mirror across from the two barber chairs.
Sports magazines and comics in the magazine
rack make me smile. And the smell of witch-
hazel. There's a black lab on the mat by the back
door that cut loose with a couple of wags when I

looked that way. It's nice to see a dog now and then. Only folks with houses and full time businesses seem to have one.

The barber behind the chair away from the front window asks me what's up. He is busy cleaning the little hairs from the neck in front of him.

"It's all good," I reply.

I pick up a comic book with some cartoon animals dressed like people on the cover. Frogs are talking to mice and bears are chasing goats; it's all a little too wild for me so I put it back and refocus on the barbers at work. It was nice to be able to come in without an appointment and just wait. One thing I like here is that time is like a warm jacket that provides for you rather than a spear that just pushes you around from one scheduled thing to another.

I felt pretty good after my haircut, and decided to walk off the main street for a while. A couple of blocks into the residential I found a little chapel, pretty in its stained glass windows. I don't consider myself a very religious person. I prefer to think of myself as spiritual, which lets me feel connected to something bigger than myself, yet not beholden to any particular rule package other than to be generally respectful. But some mornings I just feel like looking up into the universe and saying "thank you" to The One, whatever It is that unites people and people, people and animals, animals and other living things, and living things and nonliving things. I smile at the thought of being a part of That, the thing in Real Control: not the nurses nor the needle, but the Master of Moving. And dead or alive, everything's moving. Its fun to know that even when I'm dead as dirt I'll still be shooting through the solar system at over ten thousand miles per minute.

So I went in the cute little chapel on this note and found about half a dozen people sitting here and there in pews while a thin old biddy played sweet tunes on the piano up to the left of the pulpit. I thought it would be nice to think of a little sermon to share. I guess I felt pretty presentable in my new haircut. I thought for a while, and remembered a little tale I had heard in a Sunday school class long ago. I grinned to myself, and hoping I could go it, walked to the front of the chapel. When the current song ended, I quietly approached the pianist and asked her if I might share a few words. She said: "Go for it."

As I approached the pulpit I saw her take a joint from her pocket and head for the door. I guessed that she had been a cigarette smoker before, and joints often just replaced them here.

I placed my hands on the platform and spoke at a level I thought might be heard comfortably in such a small room.

"God loves you," I began. "God is love, says His

Book, so, Love loves you. And, in His world, you can be love. Love Loves Love. So much love in fact that He's made it easy to answer all life's questions. Easy as A, B, C. Well, actually, A, B, C, D. A is agape, or affection, which is what existed in the beginning. A canvas of good to paint the universe on. B is being, as He is the creator that put everything out there, including us. C is seeing, letting us know the beauty of the world that surrounds us and that we are a part of it, like a tree or mockingbird. And D is for deeds, so that we can show our membership in A universe by Being able to C the need in others and then Doing what we can to make the hurt better." I did the overhead arm letters for the A, B, C and D to get the concept across, or a cross. I looked outside and saw the piano lady was putting out her joint with wet fingertips, so I wrapped up with a modest "amen."

A couple of the folks at the rear of the church gave me a nod. A gent several years older than myself stood up and walked out with me.

"What denomination rhetoric was that, brother Glendale?"

"Well, I guess I'm a bee cee d'er. We try to put the fun in fundamentalism."

He grinned and turned to go back inside.

As I left the chapel, I was feeling pretty good. Sober and sentient. Let's go get high, I suggested to myself.

I usually get high by myself. I really do pretty much everything by myself. I like people sometimes, especially when we're doing things, but not just to sit around and chit chat. I had a friend once who was fun to chit chat with. I remember I asked him when we were kids what he liked best about girls, and he said he liked it that they came in five colors.

He told me once he had found nirvana, but came back because he got hungry.

And he said societies that don't fear hunger have sexual perversion, drug use, mental illness, and or way too fancy or way too casual clothes.

Apparently one day he got real depressed about some shitty little nothing and rather than wait for the inevitable biorhythm to lift him to a happier place, he spent the rest of his life blowing his brains out.

He would have really liked it here.

I pass by the largely singing diva house, which is what I call the tripping cabin. I haven't done it often here, and I'm certainly not in the mindset to go in now.

The first time acid did me here I was a little nervous. I had some erratic episodes in the seventies, just holding on to the trip's tail that was dragging me around the dance floor with the occasional illusion that I was leading. But the what-have-I-got-to-loose impetus that sees me through so many doubts here pushed me on ahead. I remember going into the sky building after being facially and hand scanned, going upstairs to a small, well lit auditorium with several other folks sitting or wandering around. The dose was on the back of a little rainbow stamp that I licked. Having a seat, I waited for things to happen. When I started getting the tense jaw, I got up and went into the small movie theater to the rear of the auditorium. It was about half lit and there was a movie of a rolling ocean that was a little rough for my taste but I figured I better sit down for a while to be on the safe side. The movie quickly got better. I was surging with the waves and was soon diving deep into the beautiful crystal sea. I was lost in that for a while, but then started to get busy legs. I got up and walked back into the auditorium and started to walk around. A guy came up to me and started saying something frantic but I quickly said: "Puppytalk, man, Puppytalk."

He said: "Cool," and walked away.

I didn't feel like concentrating on bullshit.

I wandered over to the art workshop and spent about fifty marvelous years finger painting an eight by ten student canvas. It was fun. At some point I kinda remember walking through the living hologram room, but it was either too far out or real that I'm very foggy on that. Actually,

I never have spoken to anyone who even remembers a hologram room, so I don't bring it up much.

I finally started getting to that coming down stage and walked outside and sat on the beachside bench and looked at the sea and its dancing waves. A nurse came around me, I think, and told me I had put my jacket on inside out. I thought it looked pretty good that way, but knew better than to argue. She helped me turn my coat around and I thanked her, noting as she went back inside that she did not seem to be making a report of this incident. Not that it mattered with a jillion cameras to watch every move everyone makes.

The next morning I woke up on the same bench feeling a little sand-caked and wretchy. Wretchy is so much better that the awful feeling of a hangover; it's just a very wide-awake self-aware state that makes you want to run away from yourself. But it's pretty easy to cure by going to the opium den to chill out the day. Which is what I believe I did that day, after a quick shower.

With the largely singing diva house well behind me, I continued my saunter. Suddenly my legs went weak and I went to one knee. It was like a chunk of my former planet has come upon me, some kryptonite robbing me of my newfound strength and confidence. It was my widow's sister coming up the path towards me, with a couple of fellows! They passed as I half kneeled there and one of the guys asked me if I was OK. I nodded and they went on.

False alarm.

Not her after all.

So much for facing everything with honesty and confidence. This was just a test, I rationalized. I'll do better next time.

I need a drink. An antidote.

No can do.

Not anymore.

I got out my pipe and took a serious hit and soon another. That was too much, of course, but I had to get away from there.

My thoughts suddenly went back to the big picture of this place. Too much thc always asks 'why are we here?'

So why are we? A lot of people think that it's just to get rid of us, or keep us cheaply. Some believe they harvest things from us when we die, like blood or corneas. One guy told me that he thought we were an experiment on how people might have to live if there's a worldwide catastrophe, like an epidemic or rogue asteroid. That set me to thinking. What would be the worst catastrophe for the human race? And it suddenly hit me like an epiphany, making my skin crawl and my head light; the worst catastrophe for mankind would be if no catastrophe at all happened. If we just keep on overpopulating by finding creative ways to defeat disease and grow food, the great white way will be elbow to elbow, with all our energy food-focused and eventually we're digging around like earthworms just trying to fill our bellies during a time of eventual food decline. As good as we are at growing more food, we are still a lot better at growing more us. There just isn't any math that could possibly make all this continue to just keep going. This was just a thought, and too real to want to consider much longer.

Maybe the nurses are an emergency management training class. Who the elite are that would run this is beyond me, but it is certainly not the AMA. It would have to be a group that has plans for not so far down the road, and probably well off the beaten path. I'll probably never know if this idea is even close, but it does inspire me to make plans that take me as far as possible from this line of thought.

With the pot rush fading, I headed for the room with the dragon's tail. Onward, into the fog.

There was a pretty large group in the den as I walked in. Quite a few were seated around a couple of tables engaged in conversation. I sat nearby and eavesdropped to see if it might be something to which I might contribute. Though a lone busker by temperament, I feel that sometimes I should engage in some mutual give and take. Fortunately, it seemed the talk was centered about something of widespread mutual interest: drugs. I turned my chair, not enough to intrude on the existing circle, but enough to show that I was part of the group.

A small brainy looking chap had the floor and was pointing out the obvious reasons for the exclusion of certain drugs from the dispensers. He apparently had already gone over the usual suspects: cocaine, heroin, speed, and the like, and was getting down on some of the less known past-the-gateway drugs.

He continued after glancing momentarily in my direction.

"And it seems obvious that there is some sort of benevolent structure in place that protects us from glue and aerosols. But perhaps if some of the more exotic drugs, like exes, were found to have a general appeal in our population, perhaps they could be added on a try and high basis. Of course, they can keep the situation static, but going along with a wave of general approval might be considered good social management. They can always retreat to the standards, but it's hard to buck the general inclination to head to higher ground."

There was a genial laugh to this obvious play on words.

A big fellow in the corner lamented the loss of alcohol, saying that with so few women about to fight over or to ride our asses about overloading, it might not be such a demon. A quick response, yeahed by a majority, was to the effect that a life without hangovers is a festival indeed.

But we have such good hangover cures here, the big fellow continued.

The brainy looking guy countered with the comment that in spite of what our tenth grade sociology teachers told us, communities are not a living beings and therefore don't need assholes. Liquor turns us into assholes.

Some light agreement and a short pause.

Another fellow ended the gap. He said that he had once chewed some khat that grows in north Africa, and found it to be pleasant and essentially thornless.

Anything from the motherland ought to be available, a chummy looking sort said. We had come to refer to Africa as the motherland, not just because all folks originally came from there, but also it was seen as more natural, like us, than the great white way.

Someone else added that khat was just like the dirt weed we used to buy for ten bucks a lid in college.

"If you want that level of high, just walk four feet behind me when I'm puffin' wax, and cop a contact high," he said.

There was another light round of approving laughter.

I was about to chime in that we already had it all; and that the grass just doesn't get any greener, but held my tongue. I recognized this as a good time to keep my mouth shut.

"Everything we say gets listened to of course, so hopefully someone will take note and take these suggestions to mind," said the original speaker. Apparently I had missed the part about the drugs in question.

Oh well, guess I'll puff what's available and then ponder the other possibilities, catching up from someone there earlier than I. So I moved to the straws and got sedated. Soon the existence of more dope in the dispensers or taverns seemed pretty superfluous, and I was just grinning at our current good fortune. I briefly thought about what my life would have been like now in the great white way, and realized I didn't give a rat's ass.

I walked down the street to the men's quarters and grabbed a blanket and pillow, made a sandwich and went back outside. I found a nice Adirondack chair and took in the closing moments of sunset. As I did, I thought about how that little gathering of citizens is about as close to government as we reach. We can suggest things, but of course there is no democracy here. Come to think of it, there may be no pure democracy anywhere anymore. Democracy is a lot like cocaine; in its pure state it is a fine and glorious entity. But the devil greed introduces the cut, which destroys the purity, the beauty and the effectiveness to such a degree that only the lowest possible elements still wish to be associated with it.

I felt myself coming down from the floaty high and was looking forward to that time when the brain is about normal again but seems to be more receptive of the things that purport to be the big answer. I got up and looked for the coffee house and located it one block over from the opium bar and park. It was atmosphere dark inside with a low ceiling and the smell of fresh coffee. I sat at a small table near a barely raised stage, where an extremely large guy was speaking some poetry. I don't know if he was reciting something old or if he was making it up as he was going along. I poured myself a cup o' joe from the small carafe on the table and watched and listened to the stageholder.

"I am the irony of my dreams
Welcoming all to our insanitarium.
We must like it; we come here often
To look at girls through testosterone glasses,
Lecturing bubbles,
And assuming tomorrow as if it were a verb.
And if this world is not heavy
How slight we must be…"

He continued to talk but I stopped paying attention.

I was enjoying the flavor of my coffee and thinking of nouns that can also be verbs. Fish…iron…flood…swing….

It seemed very important that to fully enjoy life you must focus on the verbs and leave the nouns alone. Stuff, not stuff.

I'm always amazed here at how many things you can contemplate stoned. Especially now that there's no schedule or physical need to keep in the back of your brain. The full ten per cent skittering around wherever it may.

Knowing there was none there, I checked my pocket for a quay. For no particular reason, I wanted to go quaying. I quickly reversed myself; that drug is for earlier in the day with friendly faces around, and not really a good nightcap at all.

I realized I was just sleepy. I went back to the Adirondack chair, picked up my pillow and blanket, and went inside. Even after the coffee I was asleep in minutes.

I woke up to a quiet room. I gathered myself and slipped my feet to the cool floor. I took inventory of how I was doing. My feet felt stable on the ground and flexing my knees, they felt all right too. There was a little pressure in my head. It was neither good or bad; I discovered a long

time ago that it's counter productive to label
every sensation as good or bad… most are just
life twists that deserve no moral judgment.
There was a feeling that I needed to pee; I was
going to obey that call.
I walked down the aisle between the beds and
made my way to the open plan restroom. It was
unoccupied. I walked to the wall urinal and
peed relaxingly. Then I walked to the pill
dispensary and placed my hand on the small
screen by the contents menu and pushed the
button that released a small hydrocodone pill. I
hadn't had any of those for a few days so I
figured it was the real thing and not a placebo.
Life expectancy here would sure be short if we
were given the real thing every time we had a
notion. No one here would argue that people on
drugs sometimes make bad and
counterproductive decisions.
I walked back to my bed after pilling and got the
sheet and pillow off the bed. I walked outside
and rolled onto a hammock facing the moon. I
didn't go back to sleep for a while but I didn't
mind.
I thought back to the poet I had seen earlier.
More than a few of us have put on a little weight
here. Some 'lumps in the gravy' as some like to
say. Not surprising, I guess, with food always
available, no exercise requirements, and pretty

substantial cases of the munchies. There is the opportunity to exercise, with pick-up baseball and basketball games, walking and running paths, and occasional nurse-led exercise classes in the parks. And there is what appears to be a lot of yoga, but actually some of that is just folks that have gotten too high and just ended up sitting in some unusual positions.

One thing that is a contact from the old world is food packages. We have plenty of basics here, of course, but pretty often food packages will show up in the kitchens; things like smoked salmon, prime steaks, and non-chicken birds like quail, goose and capon. They are just gifts that families back home send to no one in particular as thanks for their loved ones moving on to give younger folks a chance at the American Dream. Every once and a while a recipe will come with the food that has the notation 'Grampa's favorite,' or some such sentiment. And it does create variety and give us in the kitchen a little fun.

I remember one time I found a box in a pantry that said 'Fixings for Gary's Jamaica Beach Chicken.' Although not knowing who Gary was or which beach in Jamaica, I decided to give it a go. All that was inside the box were bags of fried pork skins and grated parmesan cheese. I followed the recipe and beat up a bunch of chicken breasts, making them pretty thin, dried them off, slathered them with mayonnaise, which we of course always have a lot of, and coated them with a sixty-five to thirty-five percent mixture of pork rinds that I had crushed to powder, and cheese. Then I put them on an oiled baking tray in the oven and cooked them on high for about half an hour. This required standing by the stove and punching the 'on' and 'high' button every seven minutes, but it turned out to be more than worth the effort. As hot grease is not allowed in the kitchens here, this is the closest thing to fried chicken we've had had since leaving America. The twenty or so people that were there made such a fuss over this crispy chicken dish that it wasn't long until pork rinds and parmesan cheese started turning up in a lot of pantries. Turns out it worked on fish, too.

I think the nurses must have some fun in putting different food combinations out for us and seeing what we come up with. A munchie mind can be downright cheflicious.

Speaking of chicken, we raise a lot of them here. There's one village, called the 'Chicken Ranch,' which raises about all we need here, I guess. For obvious reasons, it wasn't hard to get the geezers to check that village out, and once there a lot stayed. There are a lot of former farmers and ranchers over here who seem to enjoy working with the birds, and as most of them lost or quit their farms during the hard days, they enjoy doing the work without any financial pressure. This is one of those villages where the drugs don't seem to dominate; it's just a low-tech community with lots of bird talk rather than ringing phones and traffic noise. There are no barracks here, only cabins and duplexes, as this is a more stable community than some of the others down the tracks. I spend some time here on occasion when I take a break from high living; living free range with the chickens while taking in more sober conversation. We even sit around the old campfire there, and cowboy up.

I remember a story one of the old timers came up with one night after a long rain. It was a story about Noah and the flood that kinda put it in a new light. He said that before the flood, everything in the world was in black, white, and gray. People had gone bad and gotten real selfish and ungrateful in their lives, so God was gonna do away with us and return to the rule of fishes, like His own salt water aquarium. Noah begged another chance for the land dwellers and built this ark just so, proving man could live by

God's plans. After the flood, and seeing how Noah and his family cared for all His helpless creations, God gave a rainbow, the gift of colors, to the world as a promise of His glorious love. And all man had to do was say 'thank You,' every now and then.

It may not be in the Book that way, but it's just too pretty a story not to have some basis.

I was up before the sun. I took my sheets to the laundry area and quietly fixed coffee and buttered bread in the kitchen area. Walking outside, I decided to proceed with an idea that had come to me in the darkness of the early morning. Although it was still gray, I walked over to the couples' residential area and had a seat on a bench by the sidewalk. As the sun rose, and in the coolness of the morning, I began to work in a small yarden that was in obvious need of attention. Of course I could have gone to the community garden, but I was strangely feeling a need for some residential company.

Pulling weeds for long enough to make my hands sore, I walked to the water hose neatly coiled on a hook above the spigot. I gently watered the rows of lettuce, then picked up the damp weeds and took them to the compost can on the corner.

When I came back to the house, I saw a lady looking out the half opened door of the house. She said thank you, and said I could take a head if I liked. I declined, explaining I just wanted to help. She said thanks again and shut the door. No invite in this time. I went to try again.

I found another yarden in need of some attention a few houses down. Thinking I might look a little ragged, I walked back to the laundry, took a shower and got some fresh duds. Walking back to the second yarden, I planned my approach. Bending over to weed rather than getting on my knees and whistling a happy tune, this time I got results. A small fella and his gal came out to the front porch and asked if I wanted some lunch.

If it's not too much trouble, I replied.

He stayed on the porch as she went back inside.

Have a seat.

Thanks.

"Glendale, eh. I was in a Glendale, California once. Near the ocean."

"I picked it because it sounded just slightly exotic."

I wished I had said something more interesting, but I hadn't so I just went on.

"I think you have a fine yarden of carrots here."

"We've certainly had enough to share freely this year, not only with neighbors, but with the barracks too."

He looked a little self-caught, as if his statement may have been construed as a little condescending towards the single fellas.

I told him I thought it was great to share, be it the labor or the fruits thereof.

He smiled lightly.

Then his lady came out with a couple of sandwiches, saying that she would have something later.

I asked what they enjoyed doing as a couple.

He said that they liked to play golf on the nine-hole course just behind the duplex area.

"It's a lot of work to keep the fairways without tractors. But a group of us get together and do it anyway because the time spent hunting golf balls if we don't is even greater than the mowing time. And we enjoy the opium den every week or so. With our arthritis, we really make more use of the pain pills though. And we play bridge or poker with the neighbors. Nothing to bet though, and we're a little old for the strip variety."

She slapped his arm and grinned, but looked at me and straightened up.

There was a slight pause in the conversation flow.

I asked if I might use their washroom. I really wanted to see the inside of their habitation. I almost missed the nearly imperceptible glance she shot him.

"Hank, why don't you show him where the washroom is?"

I smiled at her caution. We walked into the house. It was strange how he looked larger as he entered the room, as if the enclosed space was giving him sustenance and meaning. I, on the other hand, felt smaller and phobic, as if the space would engulf me. I took this feeling and rechanneled it as a light excitement of a new adventure, better to place it in the positive category.

In the washroom I felt downright claustrophobic, but caught myself and calmed before it affected my aim.

I took care on walking back to the door not to look around too much, as not to look like I was casing the joint.

Old fears die hard.

Sometimes the world just doesn't do what you want it to.

I thanked them both for the sandwich and walked back toward town. I guess I was just out of place in the couples' world now. Probably should be. More at home in the world of…

Quay.

Why not? I thought. Not a very successful morning particularly.

So I took a pipe hit, went into the opium den, skipped the main attraction and punched the quay button on the machine. I took it and walked in a big circle outside till it had me in its clutches. When it did, I caught a big jolt of poetitis. I had the time to rhyme. I walked back in the bar. So good so far.

The crowd was thin as I walked in; in another life I would have ordered gin.

Here the best was an opium smoke that did good work just being a toke.

So I crossed to the bar and said to the man: "I'm here without money and I got no plan."

The fairly stoned bartender looked up rather distractedly. "What do you want then?"

That stumbled me but the quay caught its balance.

"A laudanum, please, to enjoy in the breeze."

"Ok, Mack."

I frowned. This should be better theatre with all the dope around. How about a little help, fella? I punched back: "I'll take the mix and head for the sticks."

The guy half-grinned and said: "Come on back when you need a fix".

I picked up the paper cup and replied: "That was hot! Thanks a lot!"

His grin grew. "Not so much, I'd lost my touch."

It's funny to hear the drugs talking to each other and the people just standing around like stick horses.

I scanned and walked outside. There was a breeze and the sweet taste of the laudanum took some of the urgency out of the quay. I wondered how many people would just stay drunk here if straight alcohol was available, and figured it would be just too damn many. I sat on a bench feeling like I was on a flat- bottomed boat in a small lake, when a guy came up and started painting a fence that ran along the sidewalk. I watched the paint dry and really enjoyed it. I started laughing until I cried.

I decided that I was really good at dope, but my people skills might need some work.

PART 2

The opium den was pretty full today, both inside and on the outside patio area. I forwent the urge to smoke first and visit later and sauntered over to sit at an outside table. There were several other gentlemen already seated there, and although I don't usually feel comfortable joining an existing group, this one was pretty casual and I didn't feel I was interrupting.

"You're just in time to hear about my big adventure last night," a tall, kinda grizzly looking gent on the other side of the table said. "Taught me a lesson I'll not soon forget. Scared the French fries outta me!"

"So go on already," proffered a really large fella sitting next to him.

"Well, I got pretty high at the opium bar late yesterday afternoon, and as I sometimes do, I took that extra step of a demerol, just thinking I would go ahead and walk to the next town on that trail over there. With that extra Demerol punch, walking a long ways comes real natural. But I started out too late to make the trip in sunlight. So there I was, higher than mister

Icarus, walking in the dark, trying to stay on the path and all alone. Well, all of a sudden my foot hits something hard and I fall for what seems like ten minutes and hit my head on something even harder. I looked up kinda groggy like and I see this light growing bigger. I think to myself, oh Lord, I've gone and died and there's that light I'm supposed to go to! So I got up and dusted off, just to be presentable, and headed towards that light that was just getting bigger and bigger. Well, I start feeling pretty convinced that I'm about to see the pearly gates, when I almost trip again, and look down at my feet. I'm standing on the gosh damn railroad tracks! I realize in a flash that that light I'm headed for has a lotta darn train behind it, so's I jump to the side just as quick as I can and barely, barely get missed by that steam roller."

We all laughed pretty good at that.

"I got up shaken, physically and spiritually, I'll tell you boys. That light nearly ate my last supper, so to speak, so the next time I think I'm at death's door, I'm calling out 'Lord, is that You or the freight train?' before I head outta the dark."

I suggested next time he could just ride the train instead of staring it down.

"I'll take that as sound advise, mister newcomer," he laughingly replied.

"My name's Pin. What's yours?"

I told him and he said: "Well, Glendale, the other

lesson is you can't always trust this place all alone. Sometimes there is safety in numbers, even if that number is low."

I asked if here were thinking of making that walk again.

"Yep" he said, "and probably in the daylight. Would you like to go? To tell ya'll a little secret, I'm on the trail of that great mystery, the City of Dreams."

I told him I had never heard of the City of Dreams.

"It's just one of those rumors us old folks like to talk about when the sky's dark and the conversation's headed no place in particular. There's supposed to be this city, you see, that's like this whole place in miniature. You choose to go in there, you can't ever go out, and you get all the answers to what this place is really all about. It's just rumor 'cause no one gets out, officially. But you know the nurses must."

I told him I thought I had seen that movie, and this place was probably not about anything except old folks having fun and keeping out of the way.

"Ah, a skeptic!" he replied. "Just the kind of sidekick I need on this journey of enlightenment! If you are right, we find nothing but fun and out of the wayedness... but if the rumors are true..."

"We'll be stuck in one spot."

"But it will be the centercut of this whole shebang!"

He was showing a lot of enthusiasm.

"Are you on a quay?" I inquired.

"Naw, just on a roll. This ain't no frat house, man. We're on a wooden boat sailing towards the edge of the world. Nobody comes back. We might as well enjoy the sea monsters as well as the sea breeze because there's no going back and reprovisioning. But I get to steer."

I made a mistake. I said why the hell not.

Pin and I walked. And walked. And walked. Away from the beach. Away from the towns on the track. Away from the track.

I asked him why he came to Opium Island.

"I was making a living and watching everyone else make a killing. The only expensive car I could ever look forward to riding in was a hearse. I just felt I was backing up and sensed a corner back there somewhere. This just seemed to be a chance at a new set of rules, like getting a chance to steal first base."

That all sounded pretty rehearsed. He seemed to be thinking of something else, but kept it to himself.

After a couple of hours he said: "Tell us a story." I considered one I thought up once on thc, the hazy cushion.

"Once upon a time somewhere in the pre-dinosaur days, when there weren't anything but bugs, an insect mom had two kids; one had its skeleton on the outside like her and one had its skeleton on the inside. The first child looked at the other fleshy sibling and saw future generations of easy to eat corn dogs. That other sibling eventually became us. But with our skeletons on the inside, we were able to get a lot bigger. They still feed on us, but they just take little bites."

After a couple of steps he looked back at me and said: "Don't tell any more stories."

We walked quietly for a while, and really got into the woods.
We were so deep in the shade that for the first time I could not feel the cameras on me.
Pin finally spoke.
"I'll tell you a story. You say that this should be a place of good theatre, and it is: the theatre of the absurd. They take the illegal and make it legal, wonderland style. They let us freely move around all the while we become neo-slaves to the pipe. This huge group of dissatisfieds comes over here and is sedated, excuse me, 'made complacent.' Sounds more like the work of homeland security than social security. Such a

blatant mechanism of control. 'Let's mainstream the ol' mainline!' Pharmaceutical fascism. Let's just hope that one day the nurses will see that they're in hospice, too, and turn the needles around on those they're in cahoots with. Like lightning, they can strike both ways."

I darn near 'puppytalked' him for not being stoned enough, but let him finish. I was glad I did. Apparently he was full of a lot more grit than grin at the moment.

We spoke little more, and travel was tough, finally a little tougher than me. So this is what it's like to be old.

"It's six hours in. I'm hungry and sober. I appreciate that we live in the land of gravy, and I'm missing it."

"Steady, boy. Look here over this ridge."

I took a few steps up a hill and looked down on what appeared to be a city out of a science fiction movie.

"There it is, comrade. The City of Dreams."

I took the view in deeply. It did not seem to be a warm and friendly village. With its structures of steel and concrete, it looked all business.

"Looks to me like we just stumbled on the control center of the whole shooting match. Just nurses down there."

I was stating the obvious.

I was getting flustered.

He confided: "A nurse told me about this city as the secret spot where all the rules are made, where the real purpose resides."

I was thinking this better not be one of those how to serve the elderly cookbook things.

"Let's get closer to the truth," he said and moved ahead.

I realized that there would be no fun here. This was the school office, and Pin obviously had no fear of the electric paddle.

"Man, I need to know what you're up to here. You've obviously hijacked me, and I want to know if you plan on flying me into a building." He looked at me for a few seconds, and then at the ground. Then back at me.

"It's hard to see through all the pot smoke, but humankind is actually a pretty brutal breed. We slap this world around like a stepchild. Your friends, the nurses, killed two of my best friends back there. And I don't need no stinking nurse's cap to kill back. I was hoping you might have some fun with me and help knock some props out from under this place. But you won't get angry. I can tell when somebody's' sold out because the truth doesn't make them angry."

Pin obviously was not the kind of guy to take inventory of what he had and figure some good place that could take him. He had sinister marrow in his bones. I knew a nurse would not have voluntarily told him about this place.

He settled down to lecture.

"Let me tell you what I think is going on; as a matter of fact I think it's pretty obvious. The folks in charge here are the folks that are hungry and sober in a fat, drunk world. The folks who watch society split into those who produce more than they consume, and those who consume but rarely produce, like us oldsters. And the glory days are ending; we're running out of stuff. There's a new car; who gets it? A couple of Americans on relief or a hard working Chinese couple that have always dreamed of one, but never had the chance? Always used to be the former, but now it's the latter. Too many Americans, being too expensive and non-productive for the world to put up with anymore. 'Take my elderly… please,' and 'What have you done for me, lately?'

So instead of just continuing to give money to those who don't do anything for the world, they may as well just sedate us, and keep the nicest ones the longest, because those are the lest expensive. Cheap, easy and effective. No more checks for the helpless from the heartless. Down and out on the one count. Society's done it to troublemakers for a long time; now they are us. Opium Island is bound to be the test case, with a heavy dose of figuring out which ones to permanently pull to be saints of the soil. And it's earth friendly; nothing's greener than pushing up daisies."

I didn't feel comfortable in the pause that followed. He looked at me intent on a response. That had obviously been his best pitch, and thinking it might be a curve, I had stepped back. He was covering a lot of territory in his hate, old foes and new.

"So you just want to kick the asses of those who rule the masses?"

Obviously annoyed at my wittiness and failure to salute, he cackled back: "Not just that, but eat them too. Being so soft, they are the most tender. I just want to get inside their hive and feast. If we don't put a fork in them today we'll be the ones plated tomorrow."

A little humorous facitiousness wasn't going to get me into his gray panther redeux.

"I don't mind rich folks driving around in mink cadillacs. I like to think I'm smarter than a martyr. Even if you're right, and making a mess down there shows you got them figured out, it doesn't matter. Ousted elites give birth to worse."

I sounded particularly coherent to myself, though I knew he wasn't getting it.

"We're geezers. Act your age."

I just threw that in as a gratuitous wild swing in a bad situation.

He hadn't given up.

"Oh, yeah, and speaking of age, what a sorry pseudo elite they've made out of us, the first

brave sheep to walk into the pen. And another thing: nothing's sadder than watching lemmings getting led to what they think is nirvana.
I'll try to fight them, not because I think I can win, but because of what they are."
"You try, I'll fly," I finished.
My Parthian shot.

I was starting to think my life might be on the line here. Not that it's not always on the line, it's just that you can't always see that's where you are.
I turned to begin the long run back towards the beach. I'll take nice and dope over assholyness and destruction.
All at damn once from behind us I heard a voice yell: "Stop, you two!"
A nurse was running up behind us, and before I could warn him off, he grabbed us both around the necks. I spun him down and watched in surprise as Pin took out a knife and stabbed the shocked nurse over and over. I reached to stop him but he pushed me back sharply. There was blood on my shoe.
"I'm not through killing him yet! Top down management, they kill my two best friends here. Bottom up management, I get two back. Take that. There goes my element of surprise, but at least we're even."
But I wasn't. He had made me a killing hand. I

guess from the moment he saw me he had my measure or lack thereof. My heart was beating fast; in another life it would have been a feeling of fear or horror, but now it was just the sensation of a real fast heart.

He looked at me coldly.

"Well, now I head to that city alone. I'll do what I can to mess things up, to put a little more fear where their consciences should be. Humanity is very good at seeing a need and then cutting the right person to length. You run, little rabbit, and good luck going back. You remember how you said you liked autumn? Well, now you're officially the fall guy. This ain't no frickin' utopia. By the way, here's a note that will explain everything."

I opened the paper he threw on the nurse's body. It said:

'Goddamn the Pusherman!'

He turned and ran and ran and ran down a small path towards the city. I guess a part of me ran with him, but it was a part from long ago.

I just started running to no place in particular. I realized I would never know for sure the purpose of this place. But it didn't matter; other people's purposes are just teases and background noise in this life I always find myself in.

I noticed my heart was still beating rapidly. I passed a large barbed wire covered gate with a small black and yellow sign on the middle of it that read 'Keep Going!' I took a few more steps in a less menacing direction, turning off to higher ground, and sensing I would never see that path again. I walked and walked, making my own way through the tangles. As I forge ahead, I notice that I'm not thinking. I start sliding out of myself and am watching me from a distance away. I'm or he's just walking, kinda unsteadily. From there I begin feeling a little dissatisfied with me, like I want to switch the channel. Nearing the steeper terrain, I fall back into myself and quicken the pace.

I come to a small clearing. Nothing around but I feel the invisible tentacles of nature all over me. I stop and take inventory. I look at my feet and see blood. It's also on my arms. My skin seems to have quit me. I am too undone to think, but try to focus. I search to remember my face but can see only the dead nurse's face in my mind's mirror. What if I am wrong about who I think I am? But it's ok; everybody probably makes that mistake.
I keep walking to higher ground.

My heart rate seems to have returned to normal as the climb steepens. I am moving through trees, trees everywhere.

I don't know why, but I've always liked these little mountain trails. I remember traveling to Colorado when I was a kid, and climbing almost to the top of a mountain and hating to come back down. And climbing to the top of sweet gum and oak trees; again I hated the retreat to the ground. So as I start up this little path, it seems like the sky is a go.

I have a sensation of moving; no pain, no desire. I realize I'm not breathing; I am only having soft memories of breathing.

The air is gone. The atmosphere abandons me.

I know I'm not dead because you're always dead before you know it.

Funny not being on drugs but feeling higher than I ever have. The stars seem so close, like I could reach up and grab one... Oh! Just did! It's hot and old and it is pulling me a trillion miles away; I'm everywhere and filling it up.

Essence of high: real and wishing holding hands and kissing.

Hello everything.
Thanks. I prefer you, too.

Out far away there is a flash of a wave that might be bigger.

The humour is off me now.

It's snowing.

About the author

Take a truck driver, bartender, newspaperman,
lawyer, teacher, health care provider and
sculptor and roll them all into one under a blue
Texas sky. It's pretty messy, but the author's in
there somewhere.